Nick and Nack
Make Music

By Brandon Budzi
Art by Jeff Harvey

HIGHLIGHTS PRESS
Honesdale, Pennsylvania

Stories + Puzzles = Reading Success!

Dear Parents,

Highlights Puzzle Readers are an innovative approach to learning to read that combines puzzles and stories to build motivated, confident readers.

Developed in collaboration with reading experts, the stories and puzzles are seamlessly integrated so that readers are encouraged to read the story, solve the puzzles, and then read the story again. This helps increase vocabulary and reading fluency and creates a satisfying reading experience for any kind of learner. In addition, solving Hidden Pictures puzzles fosters important reading and learning skills such as:

- letter and shape recognition
- letter-sound relationships
- visual discrimination
- logic
- flexible thinking
- sequencing

With high-interest stories, humorous characters, and trademark puzzles, Highlights Puzzle Readers offer a winning combination for inspiring young learners to love reading.

This
is Nick.

This is
Nack.

Nick loves to **make** things.
Nack loves to **find** things.
They make a good **team**.

You can help them
by solving the
Hidden Pictures
puzzles.

"I found a tube!" says Nack.

"Great!" says Nick.
"It will be the guitar's neck."

"How will we put it on the box?"
asks Nack.

"We will glue it to the box,"
says Nick.

Help Nick and Nack.
Find 5 bottles of glue hidden in the picture.

Happy reading!

Nick and Nack are at the park.

Nick likes the swings.

"Look how high I can go,"
says Nick. *"Whee!"*

Nack likes the monkey bars.

"Look how fast I am,"

says Nack. *"Whee!"*

Nick and Nack both like the slide.

"*Whee!*" says Nick.

"*Whee!*" says Nack.

"Look!" says Nick.

"Those drums are new."

"Listen to the beat I can make,"
says Nack.

Boom, tap, boom, boom!

"That sounds great!" says Nick.

"What else can we use

to make music?" asks Nack.

"We can make a guitar," says Nick.

"Then we can play music together."

"How can we make a guitar?"

asks Nack.

"First, we need a box," says Nick.

"I can help find a box," says Nack.

Nick finds a big box.

Nack finds a small box.

"We can use the small box," says Nick.

"Does the box need a hole?" asks Nack.

"Yes!" says Nick.

"We can cut a hole with scissors."

Help Nick and Nack.
Find 5 scissors hidden in the picture.

"Next we need a long tube," says Nick.

"I can help find a tube," says Nack.

Nack looks on the top shelf.

Nick looks on the bottom shelf.

"I found a tube!" says Nack.

"Great!" says Nick.

"It will be the guitar's neck."

"How will we put it on the box?"
asks Nack.

"We will glue it to the box,"
says Nick.

Help Nick and Nack.
Find 5 bottles of glue hidden in the picture.

"Now we need rubber bands," says Nick.

"I can help find rubber bands," says Nack.

Nack finds a rabbit.

He finds a rose.

He finds a radio.

He cannot find rubber bands.

"Here are the rubber bands,"
says Nack.

"Great!" says Nick.

"Can we paint the guitar?"
asks Nack.

"Yes, we can paint it," says Nick.
"But first, we need paintbrushes."

Help Nick and Nack.
Find 5 paintbrushes hidden in the picture.

"Now we can make our guitar!"
says Nick.

Nack cuts a hole in the box.

Nick paints the box.

Nack paints the tube.

Nack wraps five rubber bands around the box.

Nick glues the tube to the box.

"Now we can play music together," says Nack.

"Let's write a song!" says Nick.

"What notes should we play?" asks Nack.

Help Nick and Nack.
Find 5 notes hidden in the picture.

Make Your Own
GUITAR!

WHAT YOU NEED:
- Scissors
- Cracker box
- Paint
- Paintbrush
- Paper towel tube
- 5 rubber bands
- Glue

1 Cut a large circle from the front of the cracker box.

2 Paint the box and the paper towel tube.

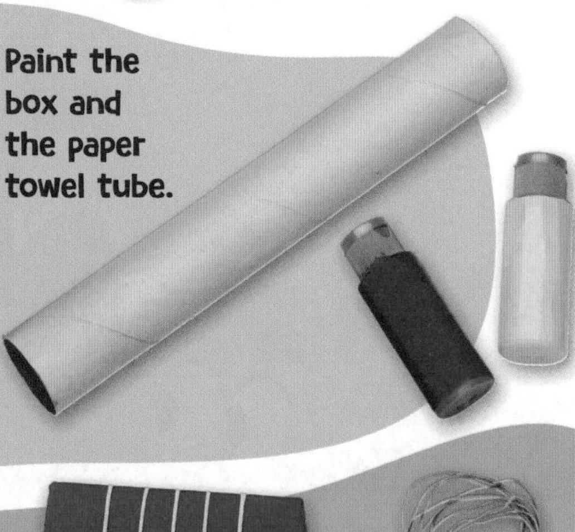

3 Stretch five rubber bands around the box lengthwise.

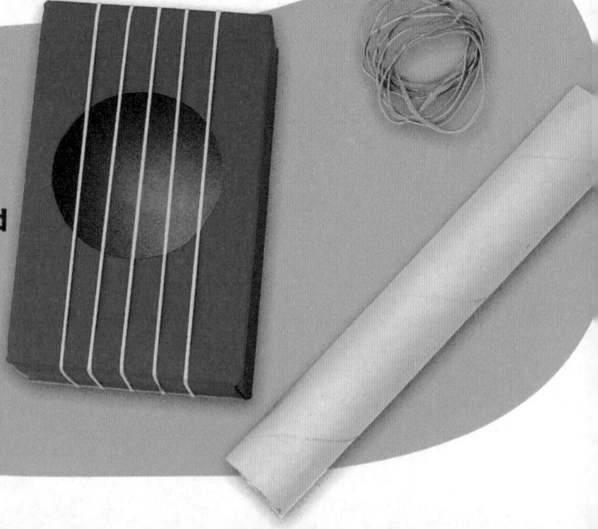

4 Cut tabs onto one end of the tube and fold them back. Use glue to secure the tube to the top of the box.

You can decorate the guitar with markers or stickers, or you can leave it plain.

Nick and Nack's TIPS

- Gather your supplies before you start crafting.

- Ask an adult or robot for help with anything sharp or hot.

- Clean up your workspace when your craft is done.

For information about permission to reprint
selections from this book, please contact
permissions@highlights.com.

Published by Highlights Press
815 Church Street
Honesdale, Pennsylvania 18431
ISBN (paperback): 978-1-64472-468-2
ISBN (hardcover): 978-1-64472-469-9
ISBN (ebook): 978-1-64472-470-5

Library of Congress Control Number: 2021938224
Printed in Dongguan, Guangdong, China
Mfg. 05/2023
First edition
Visit our website at Highlights.com.
10 9 8 7 6 5 4 3 2 (pb) 10 9 8 7 6 5 4 3 2 (hc)

Craft samples by Lisa Glover
Photos by Jim Filipski, Guy Cali Associates, Inc.

This book has been officially leveled by using the
F&P Text Level Gradient™ Leveling System.

LEXILE®, LEXILE FRAMEWORK® ,
LEXILE ANALYZER®, the LEXILE®
logo and POWERV® are trademarks of
MetaMetrics, Inc., and are registered
in the United States and abroad. The
trademarks and names of other companies and
products mentioned herein are the property of their
respective owners. Copyright © 2021 MetaMetrics,
Inc. All rights reserved.

For assistance in the preparation of this book,
the editors would like to thank Vanessa Maldonado,
MSEd, MS Literacy Ed. K–12, Reading/LA Consultant
Cert., K–5 Literacy Instructional Coach; and
Gina Shaw.